A BREW-TEA-FUL DISASTER

MERCY IGRAM MYSTERIES
BOOK TWO

LIA DAVIS

ABOUT A BREW-TEA-FUL DISASTER

Our bond was supposed to be a formality, but it's far more powerful than that...

After the magical mishap at the Merrow Tea Spot grand re-opening, Kas and I must figure out why our bond has my magic on the fritz. Our mothers say a curse was placed on both of our warring families, and our marriage is meant to usher in a truce. I have other suspicions, and an elder witch soon confirms them: this marriage is more than symbolic. It's connected to the magical rift that's kept our families at odds for generations.

As we dig into family histories, Kas and I uncover old betrayals, secrets, and magic gone horribly wrong. But every step we take to unravel the past brings us closer together—and closer to the truth behind the bad blood.

Just as Kas and I are on the verge of a breakthrough, we stumble onto something sinister. Someone is working hard to keep us apart and ensure that the feud between our families lives on. Suddenly, the rift between us feels as strong as it ever has. Now I'm terrified we'll be forced to choose between healing our clans and protecting the unexpected love we've found in one another.

1

MERCY

I was pretty sure that the only thing more dramatic than my out-of-control powers was Row swooning over our new pastry chef, Callum Burke, aka Cal. He was handsome with his baby blue eyes and caramel-colored hair that brushed his shoulders. He wore jeans, like Row and I did, with a white t-shirt under the purple Merrow Tea Spot apron.

I leaned in closer to my bestie, who was staring moony-eyed at our new employee, and whispered, "You've got a bit of drool on your chin there."

Row's cheeks flushed a rosy hue as Cal flashed her a shy, lopsided grin, nearly losing his grip on the tray of blueberry scones he was carrying. Well, it seems Row wasn't alone in her attraction. "He's just so...mysterious." Row sighed dreamily, eyes still tracking his every fumbling move.

I let out a snort of laughter. "Mysterious? Honey, that man's biggest secret is his skincare routine. I mean seriously, no mere mortal has skin that flawless."

And his baking skills. In the week he'd been here, he'd added a whole line of pastries to the tea cakes, cookies, and mini sandwiches already on the menu.

Giggles rippled from the ladies sitting at the counter in front of me. I winked at them. Row shot me a halfhearted glare, but her own laughter quickly joined the chorus. Working side by side, trading playful barbs and inside jokes with my best friend since birth, was amazing. This was our world. Our sanctuary of magical teas and community.

I turned to refill the chamomile jar, only to catch a telltale glimmer of silver darting behind the counter curtain. Narrowing my eyes, I stalked over and flung the velvet barrier aside with a dramatic swoosh.

There, looking entirely too pleased with herself, was Pippy. My pint-sized partner in crime had apparently decided my brand new silver spoon set was her own personal treasure trove. She perched atop the haphazard pile of cutlery like a queen on her throne, tiny paws still wrapped possessively around an ornate soup spoon. So, this was where all my silverware had gone.

"And just what do you think you're doing, missy?" I demanded, hands on hips in my best impression of a stern mother hen.

Pippy glanced up at me, her whiskers twitching defiantly. "I was protecting them," she declared in a dramatic squeak, her tiny paws clutching the ornate soup spoon tighter. "Do you know how many sneaky tea thieves lurk around these parts? I'm practically the hero of this establishment!"

Pressing my lips together to keep from laughing, I raised an eyebrow, crossing my arms. "A hero, huh? And what kind of hero steals from their own team?"

Her beady eyes narrowed, her voice rising in indignant protest. "Steals? Never! I'm preserving history! These spoons are relics, treasures of untold worth—someone has to ensure they're safe."

I snorted at her overly grandiose tone. "Well, Miss Guardian of the Silverware, how about you guard them from their rightful spot in the drawer instead?"

Pippy sniffed, her tail flicking with outrage. "Drawer duty is beneath my talents! You don't ask a knight to polish swords, do you?"

I grinned, finally reaching out to pluck the spoon from her grasp. "And yet, here we are. Knight or not, the tea spot has rules, Pip. No hoarding the merchandise or the kitchen tools."

Pippy grumbled something under her breath, a frequency only discernible to magical ears. Probably lamenting the indignities of being a familiar in a world where shiny objects were so cruelly withheld. I had to bite back a grin at her adorably disgruntled expression.

"Besides," I continued, setting her gently on the countertop, "I could have left you at home to spend the day with Kas and Batty."

At that, Pippy's ears drooped, a visible pout forming on her furry face. As much as she adored her winged bestie, even she had to admit that a day spent watching Kas work from home held little appeal. With a final, mournful squeak, she relinquished her hold on the spoons, allowing me to return them to their rightful place.

With crisis averted for now, I gave Pippy a consoling scratch behind the ears before turning back to the bustle of the cafe. Never a dull moment with a ferret familiar on the premises, that much was certain.

Just as I reached the front counter, the bell over

the door jingled. I glanced up and smiled at Mrs. Hawkins. Reaching up, I took a coffee cup from the shelf above the counter. "Good morning, Mrs. H."

She waved and rushed over to the last empty spot at the counter. "Morning." She leaned forward to glance at Row at the other end of the counter, checking out another customer. "Hi Row."

"Hi, Mrs. H!" Row flashed her a bright smile before turning helping another customer.

I sprinkled a little calming magic into the steaming mug of spiced rosebud tea. Giving the concoction a final swirl with the enchanted cinnamon stick, I topped the drink with frothed peppermint cream.

"Here you are." I set the violet ceramic mug in front of Mrs. Hawkins. Her eyes sparkled with delight as she inhaled the heady aroma and took a dainty sip.

"Mercy, my dear, you've done it again! This is positively transcendent." She beamed at me over the rim of her cup, her cheeks turning a rosy hue.

I chuckled and gave her a playful wink. "It's all in the magic."

Feeling rather pleased with my alchemical skills, I pivoted on my heels and reached for the dented copper kettle to pouring into a flowered teapot. I added a scoop of my new Apple Pie tea blend to the pot, then poured the hot water over it.

Instead of the expected puff of fragrant steam, a miniature fireball burst from the spout with an angry hiss. The scorching orb skittered across the polished mahogany counter straight at my hand. I jerked it back with a startled yelp as the searing heat singed my knuckles. I swore under my breath, slamming a damp tea towel over my throbbing skin.

Row rushed over. “Did you do that on purpose?”

Shaking my head, I said, “No.”

A moment later, every single teacup on the shelves suddenly sprang to life. Delicate handles morphed into flailing arms as the porcelain vessels lifted into the air, mouths gaping open in unison.

"DOOOOM!" they wailed, their high-pitched voices cutting through the usual cheery din of the cafe. "DOOOOM!"

Gasps and shrieks of alarm rippled through the crowd of patrons. I whirled around just in time to see Cal drop an entire tray of freshly baked lemon poppyseed scones. The pastries tumbled to the floor in a shower of crumbs as his face turned ashen.

In the corner, old Mr. Brooks dove behind a precarious tower of mismatched teapots, his wispy white hair standing on end. The pots teetered dangerously but somehow remained upright, as if even they were too stunned by the unfolding chaos to topple.

"Merciful heavens!" Mrs. Hawkins shrieked. Her mug crashed to the floor, splattering violet liquid across the counter.

The cacophony of screaming teacups reached a fever pitch, drowning out the panicked murmurs of the customers. I clapped my hands over my ears, my mind racing as I tried to figure out how to quell this unexpected mutiny.

"Row, A little help."

She stood in the middle of the chaos with her arms raised, frustration etched in her features. "I'm trying, but the magic is wild and not responding to me."

Suddenly, Row clapped her hands together. The noise burst through the pandemonium like a thunderclap. It sounded like a thousand agitated prairie dogs engaged in a heated debate. Everyone froze, falling into an uncertain silence, broken only by the chatter's steady rhythm.

The enchanted teacups seemed just as taken aback by this turn of events. They hovered uncertainly, handles drooping. In the momentary reprieve, a single sugar cube wobbled on the edge of the counter before plummeting to the floor. It shattered with an almost comical tinkle.

That tiny burst of normalcy was all it took to snap me into crisis mode. I vaulted over the counter and grabbed the nearest cup by its handle.

"Alright, you chipped little diva, that's enough out of you!" I growled, giving it a firm shake. The teacup let out an affronted gasp but stopped its chanting. I snatched another from the air, tucking it under my arm like a squirming toddler.

Rowan leaped down from her perch and joined the fray, coaxing the teacups into submission with a mix of soothing words and no-nonsense commands. Even Cal gingerly started picking up the scattered scones while using a serving tray as a shield.

The front door flew open with a bang. A swirling gust of wind, charged with the telltale tingle of psychokinetic magic, swept through the cafe. I glance up to see Kas standing in the doorway with his dress shirt sleeves rolled up. His artfully mussed chestnut hair gleamed under the twinkle lights strung along the ceiling. My heart stutter in my chest even as a wave of relief crashed over me.

I stared as Kas strode into the chaos of the café, all coiled power and purposeful intent. With a slight flick of his wrist, he sent the rogue teacups swirling into orderly orbits around his hand, as if he'd simply plucked the strings of a marionette. Show off.

The teacups jostled and clinked as they settled into a neat line across the counter, handles drooping in submission. Kas lowered his hand, his espresso-dark eyes finding mine across the room. A faint smirk played at the corners of his mouth.

"You okay?" Kas's low voice rumbled through me as he gently pried the tea towel from my clenched fist. I hadn't even realized I was still clutching it.

"I'm fine," I replied automatically, but my traitorous hand trembled as he ran a soothing thumb over the angry red welt marring my knuckles. Pain and pleasure sparked up my arm in equal measure.

Kas arched a knowing brow, his gaze flickering to the fading streaks of silver in my eyes. Evidence of my elemental magic at play. I fought the urge to scowl at his scrutiny, hating that he could read me so easily. No, that wasn't true. I loved my husband, but the last week hadn't been stressful. We're afraid to be intimate because the act might merge our magics together and explode our house. Okay, that might be dramatic. It was still a legit fear.

As if sensing the swirl of my emotions, Kas leaned in closer, his cedar and sage scent enveloping me. "Mercy. Let me help."

The soft words held an undercurrent of steel, a reminder of the vows that tied us together. Not just as husband and wife in name only, but as two magics irrevocably intertwined. For better or worse. I was definitely at my worse.

I sighed and forced my fingers to unclench, allowing Kas to press the lavender and mint compress Rowan had conjured into my palm. Covering it with his hand, and whispered a healing chant. The soothing spell worked its way into my skin, a pleasantly cool tingle that dulled the throbbing ache.

"Thanks," I muttered, leaning against Kas's side.

A familiar flutter of leathery wings announced Batty's arrival as he swooped through the open door to land on Kas's shoulder. He surveyed the aftermath of the teacup uprising, tiny brow ridges raised. "Well. Looks like you two have had an exciting morning."

I huffed a wry laugh, reaching out to scratch behind Batty's ears with my uninjured hand. "That's putting it mildly. I think my magic's getting worse. I hadn't reached out to Kas through the bond and it still made a mess of my shop."

Kas's eyes narrowed, and I could practically feel him rifling through my memories of the incident. Perks of being psychically linked. He wasn't doing it because he mistrusted me. He was searching for the trigger. There wasn't one which freaked me out.

"I thought we had that under control. We've all but closed off the bond." It was something neither of us wanted, but we had no choice when my magic reacted so violently when merged with Kas's.

I blew a stray curl out of my face and knelt to collect the porcelain shards scattered across the floor. My hands shook slightly as I swept up the broken pieces, a combination of residual adrenaline and magical feedback making my nerves jangle like wind chimes in a hurricane.

It had only been a few weeks since Kas and I had been forced to combine our magic through our bond to take down Edith, the vengeful witch who'd poisoned Peggy Perkins, and tried to frame me for the crime. We'd barely managed to unravel her scheme and clear my name before the High Coven could slap me with an enchanted ankle monitor that magic bound my powers. That was the last thing I wanted.

But the magical backlash of wielding that much raw power had fried my control to a crisp. The reopening of Merrow Tea Spot was supposed to be a fresh start, a chance to put that whole sordid mess behind me. Instead, it had triggered a massive surge that sent my finely honed magic into a tailspin.

Hence the fireball-spewing kettles and chanting teacups of doom.

A gentle weight settled around my shoulders, and I glanced up to see Pippy draping herself across my neck like a fuzzy, concerned scarf. She nuzzled her cold nose against my cheek, her presence a soothing balm to my frayed nerves.

"We'll figure this out," Kas said quietly, his hand coming to rest on the small of my back. My skin tingled at his touch, even through the fabric of my shirt. "You're not alone in this."

I closed my eyes for a moment, letting the truth of his words sink in. Our married and bond was still fairly new, as was our families' desire to end the centuries long feud between them. Kas and my arranged married was supposed to be the bridge for connecting all of us.

Meeting Kas's gaze, I said, "We need to figure out what this family curse is and vanquish it. For good."

He gave me a slow smile. "We will because I'm not ready to give up on us."

My heart swelled, and he pulled me close, so our bodies pressed together. Then he gave me a quick kiss. A spark of desire bloomed from the kiss, and I sighed. "I'm tired of not being intimate with my own husband, too."

He laughed and tucked a loose hair behind my ear. "We'll figure that out, too." He turned and waved his hand, throwing out a low current of magic. Within seconds, the shop was cleaned and all the customer who didn't run for the hills had fresh treats and their drinks replaced.

At least one of still had control over their powers.

I turned to Row. "I might need to take some time off until we get this figured out."

Row hugged me. "Cal and I can manage the shop.

2

The elevator doors slid open with a whisper, revealing a conference room that seemed to float above the bustling streets of Moonbeam Cove. My stomach clenched as I stepped out onto the sleek hardwood, Kas's reassuring presence at my back doing little to ease the dread pooling in my gut.

Floor-to-ceiling windows dominated the space, offering a dizzying view of the harbor far below. The late afternoon sun slanted across the polished table, glinting off the silver hair of the coven elders gathered around it. I felt like an errant schoolgirl called before the principal, my palms growing clammy as I caught sight of Andrea Ward's severe expression.

Kas's mother had always been an imposing figure

but seated at the head of the table with the weight of her authority bearing down, she was downright intimidating. Her steely gaze tracked our approach, lips pressed into a thin line that boded ill for the conversation ahead.

I fought the urge to smooth my skirts or fuss with my hair, all too aware of the way my magic crackled just beneath my skin like a live wire. It had been doing that more and more lately—surging and spiking without warning, leaving destruction in its wake. The incident with the teacups this morning was just the latest in a string of unsettling occurrences.

As if sensing my unease, Kas brushed his fingers against mine, the briefest of touches sending a jolt of calm through our bond. I clung to that steadying warmth as we took our seats, the plush leather chairs doing little to ease the tension knotting between my shoulder blades.

Andrea rang a small silver bell, the chime cutting through the heavy silence like a knife. "We're here because Mercy's magic has been spiking uncontrollably. We need answers—before the next surge does real damage."

I flinched at the words, my fingers curling into

fists beneath the table. I couldn't argue with her assessment, much as I wanted to. The raw power crackling through my veins terrified me, an untamed force I could barely hope to control.

Elder Marisol cleared her throat, drawing attention to the stack of runic ley line readings spread before her. "Mercy's power is dipping into high voltage territory. But there's no conventional buildup. It's as if her magic is resonating with something unseen."

A shiver worked its way down my spine at the ominous words. I exchanged a worried glance with Kas, seeing my own fear reflected in his dark eyes. What could trigger these surges, if not the usual culprits of emotional upheaval or external threats?

Elder Thom leaned forward, tapping a gnarled finger against the chart of my latest potion-infused readings. "No herb or hex seems to correlate," he mused, brow furrowed in concentration. "It's as if Mercy's very core is resonating with something beyond our understanding."

I swallowed hard, my mouth gone dry as dust. The elders were talking about me as if I wasn't even there, dissecting my magic like some sort of academic curiosity. It made me feel small and exposed, like a bug pinned under a microscope.

"We've hit a wall," Andrea sighed, steepling her fingers beneath her chin. "I can't find anything to confirm the rumors of a curse on our families. But I don't doubt that it's real, especially with how Mercy's magic reacted to merging with Kas's."

A curse. The word hung in the air like a specter, chilling me to the bone. Could that be the root of all this chaos? Some ancient hex long forgotten, now rearing its ugly head to tear our lives apart?

My mother reached across the table to cover my hand with hers, her touch warm and reassuring. "We're not giving up hope, though," she said firmly, holding my gaze with eyes that shone with determination. "We'll get to the bottom of this, Mercy. I promise you that."

I managed a shaky nod, throat too tight to force out the words. I wanted to believe her—needed to believe that we could find a way to tame the wild magic raging inside me before it consumed everything I held dear.

But as the meeting drew to a close, and the elders filed out with grim expressions, I couldn't shake the feeling that we were racing against a ticking clock. And if we didn't find answers soon, I feared the consequences would be more dire than any of us could imagine.

As the elders disappeared into the elevator, their ominous proclamations still ringing in my ears, I turned to find my mother and Row huddled together near the floor-to-ceiling windows. Squaring my shoulders, I crossed the room to join them, Kas following close behind.

"Row and I want to scour your attic tomorrow," I said without preamble, meeting my mother's worried gaze head-on. "To see what we can find. Row has a few spells she wants to try to locate lost information or hidden secrets."

Row nodded eagerly, her blonde curls bouncing with the motion. "I've been studying up on divination magic," she explained, a determined glint in her eyes. "If there's anything in your family's history that could point us toward answers, I'll find it."

My mother's expression softened, the lines of worry around her eyes easing just a fraction. "Of course, sweetheart," she murmured, reaching out to tuck a stray curl behind my ear. "Anything to help you both. I'll make sure the attic is unlocked and ready for you tomorrow morning."

I managed a grateful smile, leaning into her touch for just a moment. It was a small comfort, but one I clung to like a lifeline during all this uncertainty.

With a final nod of acknowledgment, Kas and I turned to leave, his hand finding the small of my back as we crossed the sleek foyer toward the elevators. The weight of his touch grounded me, a silent reminder that I wasn't alone in this fight.

As the doors slid closed behind us and the elevator began its smooth descent, I let out a shaky breath I hadn't realized I'd been holding. The adrenaline of the meeting was fading, leaving behind a bone-deep weariness that settled over me like a shroud.

Kas pulled me closer to his side. "Let's go home," he murmured, his lips brushing the shell of my ear. "We can regroup and come up with a plan of attack for tomorrow."

I nodded mutely, grateful for his steady presence at my side.

As we stepped into the foyer of our beach house, the tension of the day slowly beginning to uncurl from my shoulders. Kas moved ahead of me into the living room, his lean form illuminated by the golden glow of the setting sun slanting through the windows.

With a casual flick of his wrist, he lit the candle on the coffee table, the warm vanilla scent mingling with the crisp sea air. I inhaled deeply, letting the familiar aroma soothe my frayed nerves as I made my way to the kitchen.

It took barely a thought to summon the ingredients for a calming chamomile and lavender infusion, the herbs swirling together in a delicate dance as I heated the water with a touch of magic. The ritual of brewing tea had always been a balm to my soul, a moment of peace amidst the chaos of the world.

Mugs in hand, I padded back into the living room, the plush carpet soft beneath my bare feet. Kas had already settled onto the couch, his long legs stretched out before him and an arm draped invitingly along the back of the cushions.

I curled up beside him, letting my body melt into the solid warmth of his side. He took the mug I offered with a grateful smile, his fingers brushing mine and sending a pleasant shiver down my spine.

As we sipped our tea in comfortable silence, the soft strains of music drifted from the radio in the corner—the opening notes of my favorite song. I glanced up at Kas, a smile tugging at my lips. "Your doing, I presume?"

He shrugged, a playful glint in his dark eyes. "I might have given it a little nudge," he admitted, setting his mug aside and pulling me closer.

"Thought we could both use a bit of comfort after today."

I hummed in agreement, letting my head fall to his shoulder as I breathed in the familiar scent of cedar and sage that clung to his skin. There was something infinitely reassuring about being held by him like this, cocooned in his strength and steadiness.

Slowly, gently, his hand came up to cradle my face, tilting my chin until our eyes met. The tender expression on his face stole my breath, his gaze holding a depth of emotion that words could never fully express.

When his lips met mine, it was like coming home—a sense of rightness and belonging that suffused every cell in my body. I sighed into the kiss, my fingers tangling in the soft hair at the nape of his neck as I pulled him closer.

But as the kiss deepened, as the embers of desire sparked between us, I felt something else rise within me—a swelling tide of magic that crashed against the shores of my control.

Panic seized me as a tendril of wind whipped through the room, scattering rose petals from the vase on the mantle in a fragrant flurry. I jerked back from Kas, my heart rabbiting against my ribs as I stared at the swirling bits of crimson and pink.

"I'm sorry," I gasped, my voice thin and thready with fear. "I didn't mean to—I can't seem to control it when my emotions get too high."

Kas pulled me back into his arms, his hands running soothing circles over my back as he held me close. "Hey, hey," he murmured, his voice low and reassuring in my ear. "You're safe, Mercy. We're going to figure out how to balance this, I promise."

I pressed my forehead against his chest, focusing on the steady thrum of his heartbeat beneath my cheek. Slowly, gradually, I felt my magic settle, the unruly tendrils of wind and earth and fire quieting under his grounding presence.

"I trust you," I whispered, the words slightly muffled against his shirt. And I did—with my magic, with my heart, with every part of me that mattered.

He pressed a kiss to the top of my head, his arms tightening around me as if he could shield me from the world with the strength of his embrace alone. And for a moment, I let myself believe he could—that together, we could weather any storm that came our way.

But as the candlelight flickered and guttered in a sudden draft, an ominous shiver worked its way down my spine. The shadows seemed to lengthen, reaching out with grasping fingers to snuff out the tiny flame.

And I couldn't shake the feeling that our troubles were only just beginning.

3

The kitchen tiles were cool beneath my bare feet as I padded into the sunlit room, the smell of fresh coffee mingling with the salty ocean breeze drifting through the open windows. Row was already perched at the counter island, her fingers flying across her phone screen as she sipped from a chipped mug emblazoned with a grinning mermaid. She glanced up as I entered, her eyes still slightly puffy with sleep, and shot me a knowing smirk.

"Morning, sunshine," she drawled, her voice still husky with the remnants of slumber. "Kas is already up and at 'em, I see."

I rolled my eyes, grabbing a mug from the dish rack and pouring myself a generous dose of the dark, steaming coffee. The mornings were the only time I really drank coffee. "Unlike me, he's a morning person," I muttered, taking a scalding sip and feeling the caffeine hit my bloodstream like a jolt of electricity.

Row snorted, setting her phone down and leaning back in her chair. "He'll make a morning person out of you soon."

"Not likely."

As if on cue, Kas strode into the kitchen, his suit jacket slung over one shoulder and his tie hanging loose around his neck. His dark hair was still slightly damp from the shower, curling at the nape of his neck in a way that made my fingers itch to run through it.

He crossed the room in a few long strides, his hand coming up to cup my cheek as he brushed a kiss across my temple. I leaned into the touch, my eyes fluttering shut as I breathed in the clean, crisp scent of his aftershave.

"Heading out?" I murmured, tilting my face up to his.

"Mmm," he hummed in agreement, his thumb stroking a gentle arc across my cheekbone. "Board meeting at nine. New client. Figured I'd get in early."

I pouted, reaching up to straighten his tie. "And

leave me here all alone with only Row for company? However, will I cope?"

Kas chuckled, the sound a deep rumble in his chest that I could feel through the thin cotton of his shirt. "I'm sure you'll manage," he teased, his lips quirking up at the corners. "Just try not to burn the place down while I'm gone."

I swatted at his chest, my face scrunching up in mock outrage. "Excuse you, I'll have you know I'm a perfectly responsible adult who is more than capable of keeping our home in one piece."

He raised an eyebrow, his gaze flicking pointedly to the scorch mark on the ceiling above the stove—a remnant of my last attempt at making breakfast. I flushed, tucking a stray curl behind my ear. "That was one time," I muttered.

Kas just shook his head, his expression softening as he leaned down to press a lingering kiss to my lips. "Call me if you need anything," he murmured, his voice low and intimate. "And I do mean anything."

I shivered, my fingers curling into the lapels of his jacket. "I will," I promised, my voice coming out slightly breathless.

With a final squeeze of my hip, Kas stepped back and said goodbye to Row before heading for the door. He paused to ruffle Pippy's ears where she lay curled up on her cushion, earning himself a sleepy chirp of protest. Then, with a wink in my direction, he was gone; the door clicking shut softly behind him.

I stared after him for a long moment, my fingers coming up to press against my still-tingling lips. It never ceased to amaze me the effect he had on me even after all these months of living together. It was as if every touch, every kiss, held the same electric thrill as the first time—a crackling, sizzling energy that made my blood sing in my veins.

Row cleared her throat pointedly, jolting me out of my reverie. I glanced over to find her watching me with a knowing smirk, her eyebrows waggling suggestively. "You two are disgusting, you know that?" she teased, taking a long sip of her coffee. "Seriously, it's like living in a rom-com over here."

My cheeks heated even as a grin tugged at the corners of my mouth. "Shut up," I grumbled, settling onto the stool beside her. "Like you and Cal are any better."

Row just shrugged, unrepentant. "What can I say? The man knows his way around a pastry. It's a gift."

I snorted and shook my head as I reached for a muffin from the basket on the counter. “Ready to go?”

“Row hopped off the stool and said, “Let’s roll.”

Moments later, I climbed into Row’s black Jeep and buckled my seatbelt, breathing in the familiar scent of sandalwood incense that always seemed to linger in its interior.

"Ready for a little childhood home invasion?" Row said, scrolling through her phone to queue up one of her playlist. The opening chords of a classic rock ballad filled the car, mingling with the subtle magical humming emanating from Pippy as she perched on the dash like a fuzzy hood ornament.

As we wove through the narrow streets of Moonbeam Cove, I let my gaze drift over the quirky storefronts that lined the road, each one more whimsical than the last. It was like driving through an adorable storybook village right on the coast of Maine. I smiled as we passed the town square, where ancient oak trees dripped with ribbons and hand-painted birdhouses. This place had been my entire world growing up, and a part of me still resonated with its gentle, unhurried magic.

Pippy let out a contented squeak from her perch, and I reached over to stroke a finger down her silky back. "Not a dangerous place to call home, huh, Pip?"

Row pulled into my parents’ driveway and parked. I was barely out of the Jeep before the screen door banged open and my dad came bounding down the steps, his salt-and-pepper hair ruffled by the breeze off the ocean. "There's my girl," he said, sweeping me into a hug that still made me feel like a little kid, small and safe and cherished. It didn't matter that I just saw him yesterday at the coven meeting. I'd never turn down a bear hug from my dad.

His strong arms wrapped around me, and I breathed in that achingly familiar blend of Old Spice and sea spray, burying my face in the sun-warmed cotton of his shirt. "Hey Daddy," I mumbled, my voice cracking on the term of endearment I hadn't used in years.

If he noticed the sudden childish epithet, he graciously chose not to comment, just squeezed me a little tighter before releasing me and turning his attention to Row. "Get on in here."

Row let out a shriek of laughter as my dad enveloped her in an enthusiastic embrace, lifting her clean off her feet as she halfheartedly swatted at his shoulders. "Put me down, you big lug!" she protested, but her grin matched his for sheer wattage.

Watching the easy exchange, I felt a bittersweet warmth blossoming in my chest. My dad had always been there for me growing up, but he'd also made room in his heart for the friends and found family I'd gathered along the way. Row was like another daughter to him, and the casual affection they shared never failed to make me misty-eyed.

As Dad set Row back on her feet, he turned to usher us all inside, one burly arm slung around each of our shoulders. "Your mom headed out to Shipton with Andrea early this morning," he explained, anticipating my question before I could even ask. "They're meeting with Ava Walker to see if she has any ideas about what triggered your magical surge."

I nodded, swallowing against the sudden dryness in my throat. Ava and Drew Walker's magic bond was the same one the coven had used for my arranged marriage to Kas.

As if sensing my unease, my dad tightened his hold on my shoulders, his voice dropping into the soothing register he'd always used when I'd skinned a knee or had my heart broken as a child. "They'll find answers, sweetheart. Between your mom's tenacity and Andrea's resources, there's nothing those two can't figure out when they put their heads together."

I wished I could fully believe him, wished I could conjure the same bone-deep faith in happy endings that had buoyed me through my youth. But as Row and I made our way up to the attic to continue our own search for answers, the floorboards creaking beneath our feet like an ominous metronome, I couldn't quite shake the feeling of something ancient and malevolent hovering just beyond the edge of my vision.

A plume of dust swirled upward as we pushed open the attic door, dancing in the watery light of the single bare bulb. I coughed, waving a hand in front of my face as my eyes adjusted to the dim, close confines of the space. It smelled of mothballs and old secrets, the kind of place that might house a colony of ghosts alongside its cobwebbed relics.

Row made a soft sound of surprise beside me, her gaze sweeping across the jumble of antiquities that crowded the narrow room. Battered steamer trunks lined the slanted walls, their leather sides scuffed and peeling with age. Faded portraits of stern-faced ancestors peered down at us from ornate gilt frames, their eyes seeming to follow our every move with silent judgment.

I shivered, rubbing my arms against the sudden chill that had nothing to do with the temperature. There was something unsettling about being surrounded by the detritus of my family's past, as if the very air was thick with the weight of unspoken histories.

Row wasted no time in murmuring an incantation for a location spell, and suddenly, thin tendrils of pale blue light snaked across the floorboards, up the walls, and over the jumbled heaps of boxes. The eerie glow threw the contents of the attic into stark relief, illuminating faded labels and worn embellishments.

"A basic seeking spell," Row explained with a grin, tucking her wand back into her pocket. "It should help guide us to anything that might apply to your...situation."

I nodded and watched the luminous threads of magic twined around the legs of an ornate armoire. The treads pulse faintly as they highlighted a trunk with "1872" stamped across its lid in peeling gold leaf. Another strand dipped into a crate marked "Ward Heirlooms," while a third danced over a hatbox labeled "Ingram Ceremonials".

But it was the object in the far corner that drew my gaze like a lodestone, the shimmer of Row's spell almost seeming to coalesce around it in a halo of spectral light. Draped in a moth-eaten blanket were the edges of a large, leather-bound book, its spine cracked and weathered with age.

Picking my way carefully through the maze of boxes and old furniture, I reached out to lift the fabric, my breath catching in my throat as I revealed the book in its entirety. The cover was a rich, burnished mahogany. The double crest embossed on its surface was still clearly visible. The crest was intertwined with sigils of the Ward and Ingram families, their edges worn smooth by passaging countless hands.

"Elara Ward's grimoire," I breathed, my fingers hovering reverently over the ancient tooling. "Row...this could be the key to everything."

Gingerly, I lifted the heavy tome and carried it to a spindly legged side table. The book fell open in my hands as if eager to divulge its secrets, releasing a puff of air that smelled of parchment and dried herbs. And perhaps just the faintest whiff of smoke—an echo of its mistress's favored element.

I scanned the cramped handwriting on the yellowing pages, my heart beginning to pound as I glimpsed mentions of "elemental magics" and "the great rift betwixt the families." But it was the entry nearly two-thirds of the way through the book that made my blood run cold, the ink marring the page, the rusty brown of day-old blood.

"1872," I read aloud, my voice shaking. "The bond-forging." The words ignited a spark of recollection in my mind, my mother's stories of the ill-fated ritual meant to heal the ancestral feud swimming to the surface. But those stories had been little more than whispered legends, their edges softened by time and careful editing. They hadn't carried the visceral horror embedded in Elara's recounting.

"We attempted the merge by the light of the Wolf Moon. But the elemental and psychokinetic magics would not be easily tamed. As Marcus spilled his blood into the chalice, the sky split with unholy fire. The flames danced grotesquely as they consumed the altar, ribbons of blood and blackened ash swirling on the wind."

I swallowed hard, my stomach churning as I scanned the next few lines. *"It was as if the very gates of hell had opened to spew forth their most profane occupants. The blood ritual was meant to join, but some malevolent force sought to rend asunder..."*

The page ended in a violent slash of ink; the words giving way to a ragged tear that bisected the parchment. Whatever Elara had witnessed that night had marked a turning point from which there could be no return.

Shaken, I turned to the next page, hoping for some clue to help interpret the ghastly scene. But there was only a small, cryptic notation in the margin, squeezed between a diagram of the phases of the moon and a list of ingredients for a poultice to heal broken bones.

"Should the ancient blood bond ever fail, seek the counsel of the elder witch Nina Moon. She alone knows the truth of what transpired, and how it might yet be set right."

I was just about to turn to face Row when a flicker of movement in my peripheral vision made me freeze. In the tarnished surface of an old full-length mirror propped against the slanted ceiling, I thought I glimpsed a dark shape flit behind my own reflection, there and gone between one blink and the next. Heart in my throat, I whirled to face the shadows that pooled in the eaves behind me, half expecting to find some corporeal specter reaching out with grasping hands.

But there was nothing there. Only the dancing motes of dust caught in the feeble light of Row's seeking spell, and the ragged sound of my own breathing in the preternatural stillness.

"Mercy?" Row's voice was tentative, worry etching itself between her delicate brows as she crossed to my side. "What's wrong? Are you alright?"

I shook my head, not quite trusting myself to speak past the dryness in my throat. My heartbeat thudded in my ears. I couldn't be certain whether what I'd seen had been a trick of the light, an illusion conjured by my own unraveling magic, or something much, much worse. But I knew I couldn't dismiss it.

Row's slim fingers closed around my wrist, her touch grounding me even as her voice lifted in a weak attempt at levity. "Don't tell me your magic is playing tricks on you again. It's not nice to spook your best friend when you've lured her into a dusty old attic to go rummaging through your family's eldritch heirlooms."

I forced a laugh, but it sounded brittle even to my own ears. "I'll be sure to have a stern talk with it about its sense of humor."

But even as I tried to match Row's lighthearted tone, I couldn't shake the bone-deep certainty that we were being watched. That some malevolent force had noted our attempts to unravel the curse's origins, and even now lurked just beyond the veil, biding its time.

The feeling clung to me like a second skin as we packed up the grimoire and made our way back down the narrow attic stairs, our shadows thrown long and distorted against the peeling wallpaper. It followed me out into the thin autumn sunlight, an invisible weight bearing down on the back of my neck as we said our goodbyes to my father and climbed back into the Jeep.

And it coiled tighter still as we merged onto the coastal highway that would take us back to Moonbeam Cove, the taste of salt spray mingling with the acrid tang of foreboding on my tongue.

Whatever waited for us in the woods beyond the town limits, whatever grim purpose Advisor Nina had for us, I knew one thing for certain - the dark shape in the mirror had been no figment of my imagination. It had been a warning, a harbinger of the ancient forces stirring to life in the wake of my unbalanced magic.

And if we didn't break the curse before the blood moon rose, I had a feeling it would be more than just my own reflection I'd see swallowed by shadow.

4

The next morning, Kas and I sat at the breakfast nook. Sitting back in my chair, I cradled a cup of chai tea, watching Kas thumb through the journal I found in my parent's attic.

"Someone sabotaged Elara's ritual. But who? And why?" I said after several long moments.

Kas set his mug down with a thoughtful hum and reached for his laptop. He flipped it open, the glow of the screen illuminating the sharp angles of his face. I watched, mesmerized, as his hands flew across the keys, his brows furrowed in concentration.

Fifteen seconds later, a slow grin spread across his face, revealing the dimple in his left cheek that never failed to make my heart stutter.

"Nina Moon," he said, turning the screen toward me. "Lives in a massive treehouse up in the foothills."

I leaned in, scanning the search results with widening eyes. A few more keystrokes, and he had her exact coordinates pinned on a satellite map, the location pulsing like a beacon.

"Well then," I said, draining the last of my latte in one scalding gulp. "What are we waiting for?"

We loaded into Kas's midnight blue Range Rover, the leather seats still warm from the late afternoon sun. Pippy and Batty scrambled into the back, their excited chatter filling the air.

Kas turned the key, the engine purring to life with a throaty rumble that sent a shiver down my spine. We wound our way out of town, the bustling streets giving way to jutting granite. Salt-tinged breezes whipped through the open sunroof.

"If Nina can decode Elara's margin notes," I said, my voice nearly lost beneath the rush of the wind, "maybe we'll learn who planted the binding curse. And how to break it."

Kas glanced at me sidelong, the dying light painting his profile in shades of gold and shadow. In the rearview mirror, I glimpsed Pippy and Batty, locked in a polite tug-of-war over a peppermint stick.

I wasn't even sure where they found that because Kas keep his car clean to the point of obsession.

The sight made me smile despite the gravity of our mission. There was a strange sort of comfort in their playful antics, a reminder of the life and laughter that persisted even in the darkest of times. But beneath that warmth lurked a flicker of unease, a prickling at the nape of my neck that I couldn't quite shake. It felt like the magic itself was shifting, gathering like the electricity before a storm.

I flexed my fingers against my thighs, feeling the power hum just beneath my skin. It was getting stronger each day, harder to control. I could only hope that Nina held the key to containing it before it consumed me completely.

The trailhead parking lot was empty when we arrived. Kas pulled into a spot near the edge, the tires crunching over twigs and dried needles.

I stepped out into the cooler air. Taking a steadying breath, I reached for Kas's hand, our fingers tangling together like roots. With Pippy wrapped around my the back of my neck and Batty flying beside Kas, we started up the trail.

The deeper we ventured into the moss-carpeted woods, the more I felt like I was crossing into another realm entirely. Shafts of honeyed light slanted through the canopy, dappling the undergrowth with pools of molten gold. The air grew thicker with each step, rich with the loamy scent of bark and fern and ancient magics.

A flash of movement caught my eye through the lacework of branches, and I looked up to see towering platforms strung between the trunks of the largest oaks like massive spiderwebs spun from timber and dreams. Rope bridges swayed in the breeze, connecting the sprawling levels of Nina's magnificent treehouse. Lanterns dangled from the eaves, not yet lit but already glowing with the promise of hidden delights.

Batty let out a trill of wonder, his wings fluttering with eagerness. In a blink, he took off toward the staircase spiraling up the nearest tree, a pinprick of black darting through the greenery. Not to be outdone, Pippy gave an affronted squeak and scampered down my back so she can jump to the ground. Then she ran after him.

Kas and I exchanged an amused look as we followed our familiars up the porch steps, the weathered wood creaking beneath our feet. Even with the weight of our mission pressing down on us, it was impossible not to be charmed by their playful antics.

We reached the top and stepped out onto a broad

deck that seemed to float among the rustling leaves. I turned a slow circle, my breath catching at the view of the forest canopy stretching out to the horizon. Wind chimes tinkled from the overhanging branches. The air was sweet with the scent of lavender and wild honey.

Kas crossed to the carved rune doorframe, raising a hand to rap against the stained oak. But before his knuckles could land, the door swung inward with a whisper of welcome.

Nina Moon had a timeless quality to her. Her silvery fell in soft waves to her waist. Her eyes were a pale blue, seemed to hold thousands of years' worth of secrets in their depths. She wore robes the color of a midnight sky, embroidered with the glimmering threads of constellations.

"Welcome, Mercy Ingram and Kas Ward," she said, her voice like honey poured over crackling embers. "I've been expecting you."

My skin prickled with awe and the slightest tinge of unease as I met her gaze. There was power there, ancient and vast, thrumming just below the surface. In that moment, I knew beyond any doubt that if anyone could help us unravel the curse that had snared our families, it was her.

A soft chitter drew my attention to a shadowy

corner of the room, where a creature emerged on delicate, inky paws. It took me a moment to register the creature was a raccoon, but one unlike any I had ever encountered. Its fur was a sleek ebony, interrupted only by intricate silvery markings that swirled across its back like wisps of starlit smoke.

"This is Zuri," Nina said, extending a hand to the beautiful creature. It padded over to her without hesitation, leaning into her touch as if they shared one heart, one mind. "My beloved familiar and dearest companion."

I couldn't help but stare in wonder as Zuri turned to regard Pippy and Batty, who had frozen comically mid-wrestle on the intricately woven rug. The raccoon familiar crossed to them slowly, her bushy tail swaying. It stretched out its muzzle, delicately sniffing first Pippy, then Batty, as if taking their measure.

Whatever Zuri sensed must have passed muster, because in the next instant, she let out an inviting chitter. Pippy and Batty collectively scrambled to their feet with no shortage of enthusiastic squeaking. Zuri flicked an ear, then turned and ambled deeper into the treehouse, clearly expecting them to follow. With a final glance back at me, Pippy galloped after her new friend, Batty swooping along behind.

A sudden flare of worry tightened my chest as I watched my familiar disappear down the curving hallway. It was rare for Pippy to leave my side since she was so young—she was only a little over a year old—especially in unfamiliar surroundings. The urge to call her back, to keep her close, pulsed through me like a second heartbeat.

But before I could give voice to my unease, Nina laid a gentle hand on my arm, her touch seeming to leach the tension from my muscles like a poultice drawing poison from a wound.

"Be at ease, Mercy," she murmured, a knowing glint in her eyes. "Zuri is simply taking them to her den to get better acquainted. No harm will come to them under this roof—you have my word."

I swallowed, forcing a nod. "Of course. I'm just not used to having Pippy out of my sight these days." A wry smile tugged at my lips as I glanced at Kas. "Though I suppose I should be glad they have their own space back at home. Pippy and Batty's room is practically a wild playground at this point."

Nina's eyes crinkled with humor even as a solemn understanding passed between us. If Pippy was content to explore this enchanted space with her new companions, then I would simply have to trust in the bond we shared.

Drawing in a steadying breath, I turned back to face Nina fully, feeling the weight of her ancient gaze settle on me like a mantle. "We've come to ask for your help. There are...forces at work in our lives, dark magics stirring that we don't fully understand."

I withdrew Elara's journal from my satchel, handling it with reverent fingers. "We found this hidden among my family's most secret histories. It speaks of a ritual gone wrong, a curse planted like a seed in the bloodlines of our ancestors."

Kas shifted closer, his shoulder brushing mine in silent support. "The margin notes mention your name specifically. That you might hold the key to deciphering what truly happened that night."

Nina accepted the journal with a nod, her eyes scanning the spidery script as if reading a language only she could parse. A frown gathered between her brows, deepening with each passing heartbeat.

"This is dire knowledge indeed," she murmured at last, a shadow passing behind her eyes like clouds before the moon. "A story I had hoped was merely a whispered legend. But if the curse is quickening in your blood, then perhaps the time has come to unearth the truth."

She raised her gaze to pierce me with eyes gone pale as sea glass, sending a shiver racing down my spine. "But be warned, child. The secrets buried in your families' past may be more tangled and treacherous than even I can fully unravel. I will do all in my power to guide you on this path...but the final steps maybe yours to take alone."

My mouth went dry at her words, a cold finger of dread trailing up the back of my neck. In that moment, I felt the full weight of my legacy pressing down on me. But beneath the fear, beneath the icy coil of uncertainty, a flicker of determination took root in my chest. A spark that whispered this was my birthright, my battle to wage. And with Kas by my side and Nina's wisdom to light our way, perhaps we stood a chance of vanquishing this darkness once and for all.

Squaring my shoulders, I met Nina's timeworn gaze with a fire of my own. "Then let us begin."

Nina's gaze bored into mine, ancient and fathomless as the heart of the sea. I felt pinned beneath the weight of her scrutiny, like an insect trapped in amber. Her eyes flicked to the curling silver threaded through my own. It was like she was looking through me, into me, as if sifting through the snarls of my bloodline for hidden secrets.

"Just as I feared. The surge in your powers isn't random," she murmured at last, her voice like leaves skittering over forgotten graves. "It's the bloodline curse accelerating. Your elemental core is resonating with the old binding magic Elara performed that would serve as a witch's treaty. A truce, but as she explains in her journal didn't work."

"Because someone sabotaged the ritual." I'd told Kas that before we left our house. Hearing Nina confirm it made it so much more real.

Nina turned away, drifting toward a workbench in the far corner of the living room, laden with dried herbs and gleaming vials. I caught the sharp green scent of crushed rosemary, the honeyed whisper of wild chamomile, and beneath it all was the cold mineral tang of stone and deep earth.

"Mercy," Kas said softly from beside me, his fingers brushing my wrist. "Breathe."

I hadn't realized I'd been holding myself so rigid. I let out a shuddering exhale as we watched Nina work. She swept herbs into a mortar. Next came a pinch of bone ash, crushed to a fine grey powder that seemed to leach the color from everything it touched. Finally, a sprinkling of moonstone dust, shimmering like captured starlight.

Nina's lips moved soundlessly as she combined the ingredients, her low chant rising and falling like ocean waves against the shore. A plume of iridescent mist bloomed from the bowl, curling around her hands as she kept grinding, kept stirring. The heady perfume thickened, cloying and dark and wild.

With a final word that shivered against my skin, Nina poured the shimmering liquid into a waiting chalice. The pewter flagon seemed to drink in the light until only a faint violet sheen remained. She held it out to me, her expression unreadable.

"Drink."

I took the chalice with numb fingers, the metal searing cold against my palms. I could feel the magic humming within, a low and unsettling resonance like the drumbeat of an approaching army. Kas's hand settled at the small of my back, warm and steadying.

Bracing myself, I brought the cup to my lips and drank.

The taste hit me like a physical blow. It tasted like burnt herbs and grave soil and the copper tang of old blood. I gagged, the potion scouring my throat as it went down. It settled in my belly like a cold stone, radiating icy tendrils through my veins until I couldn't tell if I was shivering or burning up from the inside out.

Nina's fingers brushed mine as she took the chalice, her skin fevered against my own. She raised it to her mouth and sipped, her face contorting with the same visceral revulsion I'm sure had just twisted my own features. A strangled sound that might have been a laugh escaped me. How absurd to be standing here in a fairy-tale treehouse, bonding with an ageless witch over the world's worst cocktail.

As Nina set the cup aside, her eyes met mine, and any spark of mirth withered under the gravity of her stare. "That balancing spell you drank will hold the surges at bay. For now. But do not attempt to merge your magic again until you find the catalyst."

"Catalyst?" The word rasped against my raw throat, my tongue still burnt-numb from the potion.

In answer, Nina turned back to Elara's journal, still lying open to the passage I'd discovered. She laid her palm flat against the crackling leather, fingers splayed. As I watched, the faded ink seemed to shimmer, rearranging itself into new patterns beneath her touch.

"An amulet," she murmured, voice distant. "It's hidden. It anchors the curse, channels its malignant energies." Her finger tapped the margin of the page, where a cramped footnote glowed a coppery red. "High tide at the chapel ruins, where the ritual was performed."

My heart hammered against my ribs, a drum line for rising dread. I swayed on my feet, unsteady, and felt Kas's hand come up to rest at the small of my back. An anchor of my own as Nina's words crashed over me.

"The amulet," I managed, my voice a tattered wisp. "We find it...and then what? Destroy it?"

Nina lifted her head to meet my gaze, the candles throwing the lines of her face into stark relief. In that moment, she looked impossibly old, a creature of time's slow erosion. "You sever the connection, cut the rot from the root. But be warned..." She raised a hand, and I fell silent. "The amulet is a manifestation of Calrix's corruption. A talisman of her malice given form."

I blinked, thrown. "Calrix?"

Nina glanced away, her yellowed fingers tracing the whorls of the grimoire's spine. "The sorceress who perverted the binding ritual meant to unite the two families centuries ago. But what most do not know is..." She leaned closer, the sweet-sour reek of her breath fanning across my cheek. "Calrix did not perish that night, as history would have us believe. Elara's notes speak of an enduring evil, one that could conceal itself unnaturally to walk among the living, wearing a face not its own."

I reeled back, bile climbing my throat. "You're

saying that Calrix could still be out there? Hiding in plain sight?"

Nina tilted her head, a strange light in her eyes. "I think she may yet walk among us, disguised in flesh and blood."

Like a corporal ghost? I didn't dare ask that out loud. I wasn't sure I wanted to know right that second.

Kas and I were silent as the grave on the drive back home, hands clasped between us over the console. Our familiars were a whirlwind of chatter in the back seat. Every shadow seemed to flicker with unnatural movement in my peripheral vision, every rustle of leaves in the night wind carrying a whisper of dark promise. I rolled my window down an inch, hoping the rush of cool air would clear my head. But if anything, it only heightened the smell of loam and secrets, the scents of the forest chasing us even as we left it behind.

At last, Kas squeezed my hand, breaking my spiraling thoughts. I blinked over at him, taking in the tension in his square jaw, the furrow between his brows. "What is it?" he asked softly, eyes still on the winding road ahead. "You're thinking so loud I can practically hear it."

I swallowed, the lingering rasp of the potion still

coating my throat. "I can't shake this feeling like someone—or something—is watching us."

In the murky dark of the oncoming night, the trees seemed to crowd closer, branches grasping. Kas' eyes met mine in the flash of a passing car's headlights, shining with reflected worry and resolve. In silence, he lifted our joined hands, brushing a kiss against my knuckles.

A promise and a prayer, whispered on a road that felt like a slow descent into an all-consuming darkness.

5

The crunch of gravel under the Ranger Rover's tires felt far too loud as we pulled into our driveway. I let out a breath, my fingers aching from how tightly I'd been gripping my own arms as if I could physically hold myself together. Beside me, Kas cut the engine and the swelling darkness rushed in to press against the windows, a living thing hungry for the feeble sanctuary of the car's interior.

He reached across the center console, took my hand, and pried my white-knuckled fingers from around my biceps. I shuddered at the warmth of his skin, the steadiness in that simple touch tethering me to some semblance of reality.

"Come on," he murmured, thumb stroking

soothing circles against my chilled flesh. "Let's get inside."

I managed a jerky nod, shoving the car door open with leaden limbs. The scuff of my feet against the concrete seemed to echo around us. I shivered as Kas hurried ahead to unlock the front door, the porch light limning the carved lines of his face.

A flash of movement caught the corner of my eye and I whirled, heart leaping high into my throat. But it was only Pippy and Batty, darting past us into the house.

Kas lifted a brow at me, the soft click of the door snicking shut behind us sounding impossibly final. "You okay?"

I swallowed, my pulse still thudding erratically at the base of my throat. "Yeah. Just...jumpy."

It was such a pitifully inadequate description for the maelstrom of sick dread swirling in the pit of my stomach, but Kas just nodded, his expression softening in understanding. He gathered me to him in the circle of his arms, solid and warm, and I let myself collapse against the steady bulwark of his chest. He smoothed a broad hand up and down the knobs of my spine, the calluses on his palm catching on the thin jersey of my shirt. I turned my nose into the crook of his neck, breathing deep of the salt-sage-cedar scent of him, letting it ground me in the here and now.

"We're going to figure this out," he murmured against my temple, a grim thread of promise under the gentle rasp of his voice. "We *will* break this curse and stop Calrix, whatever it takes."

I wanted so desperately to believe him, to wrap myself up in the certainty of his words like armor against the encroaching darkness. But even as I clung to the comfort of his embrace, I couldn't quite shake the viscous dread trickling down my vertebrae, the bone-deep knowledge that Calrix's evil had slept like a seed in my blood for generations. That it would stop at nothing to see its dark designs come to fruition.

Drawing a shuddering breath, I pulled back just far enough to meet Kas's eyes, my fingers curling into the front of his shirt. "I know we will," I said, hoping he couldn't hear the waver in my voice. "But first we need to figure out what the hell her actual plan is."

His mouth thinned to a grim line, understanding and shared frustration flickering in the depths of his gaze. With a short nod, he released me and shrugged out of his coat. "Go get comfortable," he said, toeing off his boots. "I'll throw together a quick dinner, and then we can settle in and try to piece together whatever we can from Elara's journal."

The familiarity of our nightly routine was seeping back into my muscles, my body moving on autopilot to hang my jacket on its hook, to line my sneakers up beside Kas's larger ones in their cubby. After using the restroom and washing up, I drifted into the kitchen in his wake, moving to fill the kettle for tea. The motions were soothing, almost hypnotic.

I watched Kas work from the corner of my eye as he assembled sandwiches, the bunch and flex of his forearms mesmerizing in my exhausted haze. He glanced up, catching my gaze, and his lips quirked in a tired but genuine smile. The lines around his mouth and eyes seemed deeper than they had yesterday, grooved with new tension, but the naked affection in his expression made my heart clench.

After we ate and fed the familiars, I grabbed Elara's journal before we went into the living room to curl up on the couch. I pulled my legs up beneath me, leaning into Kas's side as he wrapped an arm around my shoulders and tugged me more snugly against him. With his free hand, he snagged a throw off the back of the couch.

I stared at the journal in my lap for a long moment, gnawing on my lower lip, before blowing out a harsh breath and flipping it open to where Nina's guiding magic had decoded the crucial pages.

Kas shifted behind me, turning so that he sat sideways on the couch with one long leg stretched out along the cushions and the other foot braced on the floor. With gentle pressure on my hips, he maneuvered me back against him so that I was cradled between the V of his thighs, my spine flush to his broad chest. His warm breath on the back of my neck as he hooked his chin over my shoulder, reaching around me to spread the journal open wider.

Together, we pored over the script, murmuring salient phrases aloud between us. With each turned page, the true scope of Calrix's ancient betrayal took shape. My breath caught in my throat as Elara detailed the sorceress' foul machinations. How she had perverted the ritual meant to heal the rift between the families, laying her curse like a malignant seed in the bloodlines of our ancestors. How it was meant to stop all future bonds.

"She planned this." Kas's growl rumbled through me, sharp with remembered rage. "Our binding ritual was never meant to mend anything. It was just a means to an end. A way to keep the curse tied to our families, siphoning power until the day her chosen vessel ascended."

Chosen vessel. The phrase sent a sick shudder rolling down my spine. It didn't take a magical scholar to figure out just who Calrix had selected as the unwitting key to her dark designs.

But before I could spiral too far down that black rabbit hole of despair, Kas stiffened behind me, his arm tightening reflexively around my waist. "Son of a bitch," he bit out, his voice gone flat with shock. "I think I know who she is."

I twisted in his embrace, my brow furrowing as I tried to parse his sudden shift in focus. "What? Who do you mean?"

"Calrix." Kas stabbed a finger at the open journal before grabbing for his phone on the side table, all coiled intensity now as he typed furiously. "I thought the name sounded familiar, but I couldn't place it. Until now."

He spun the phone around to face me. The screen filled with an employee profile from the Ward Industries internal directory. The woman smiling blandly up at me had an ageless sort of beauty, her pale blonde hair twined into an impeccable chignon at the nape of her swanlike neck. But it was her eyes that snared me—a piercing, eerie blue that seemed to look through the screen and pin me in place.

"Dr. Clarice Moorland," Kas bit out, each word dripping venom. "One of the top magical researchers on the payroll. She's been working for us for years, consulting on everything from ward schematics to theoretical thaumaturgy."

He shook his head, disgust twisting his mouth. "I can't believe we didn't see it sooner. The breadcrumbs were all there. Her uncanny knack for turning up right when we needed her expertise, the way she always seemed to steer us toward the darker applications of magic..."

"She's been playing us," I realized, nausea rising thick and sour in the back of my throat. "Biding her time and pulling our strings until the moment was right."

Kas nodded grimly, the tendons in his jaw standing out in sharp relief as he clenched his teeth. "And I have a sinking feeling that moment is coming up fast. Look at this."

He flipped back a few pages in the journal, tapping an entry from mere days before the warped binding ritual. Elara's usually meticulous handwriting was nearly illegible here, the quill strokes erratic and splotched as if her hand had been shaking.

"An ascension ritual," I breathed, the words tasting like grave dirt on my tongue. "Do you think that's what this has all been building toward? What Calrix is planning?"

Kas let out a slow, controlled breath, his arm like an iron band around my middle. "It would track with everything else we've pieced together. She's been siphoning power through the curse for generations, storing it up like a battery. And now, with your magic surging out of control..."

He didn't need to finish the thought. We both knew I was the key—the spark that would ignite the powder keg Calrix had been packing for centuries. My unpredictable, wild magic was the final piece she needed to ascend from her wraithlike half-life and retake corporeal form.

And if she succeeded, it wouldn't just be our families and Moonbeam Cove that paid the price. It would be the world.

I closed my eyes, trying to bring my breathing under control as my pulse thundered in my ears. Kas's arms tightened around me, his large hand splaying across my stomach as he pulled me back more firmly against him. I focused on the solid heat of him, the gentle rasp of his calluses catching on the thin cotton of my shirt. The way the clean salt and cedar smell of his skin filled my head, pushing back the clawing edges of panic.

He had become my anchor, the steady keel keeping me from capsizing entirely as the magnitude of what we were facing crashed over me in drowning waves. As long as I had him beside me, I could weather this. We could weather this. Together.

Blowing out a shaky breath, I reopened my eyes, my gaze falling on the journal. Slowly, I reached out to trace the sigil embossed on the cover, the pad of my finger following the swooping lines of the Ingram crest twined with its Ward counterpart. Two halves of a whole. A reminder of the ties that bound us, for better or worse.

"Then we'd better figure out how to stop her," I said simply, the words ringing with a conviction I wasn't entirely sure I felt. "Before she can finish what she started all those years ago."

Kas kissed my temple. “Then let’s go to the chapel and find that amulet.”

6

A few minutes later, we peeled out of the driveway, heading to the chapel. I couldn't shake the surreal sense of déjà vu. How many times in the last few days had we careened down this winding road into the jaws of the unknown?

But this time was different. This time, we weren't fumbling blindly in the darkness, hunting for bread-crumbs and cryptic clues. This time, we knew how our enemy was. We knew what we had to do.

The beam of the headlights carved through the coastal mist like a blade, illuminating snatches of the familiar road in stuttering flashes. Twisted cypress trees, their branches gnarled like arthritic fingers. Moonbeam Cove's cheery welcome sign, the painted letters peeling and faded. And there, in the distance, the jagged silhouette of the chapel ruins rising from the cliffs.

As we drew closer, the perversion of sacred ground was almost a tangible force. The mist curled around the crumbling stones, less a natural phenomenon and more than a miasma belched up from the putrid depths of the earth. By the time we reached the foot of the weed-choked path, the hairs on the back of my neck were standing at full attention, every instinct screaming to turn back.

We had come too far to turn around now. The amulet hidden within those dank walls was the key to unraveling Calrix's curse, the noose she had strung around the neck of our family lines. Whatever shadow-steeped horrors lurked in the bones of the chapel, I would gladly face them head-on if it meant a chance to break the family curse.

Kas parked the Range Rover and killed the engine, the sudden silence pressing like a physical weight. Without a word, we got out of the car and carefully walked up the overgrown path. The ruined arch gaped before us like a mouth. The dark energy seeped from the cracks in the masonry.

The shadows inside the chapel ruins pooled in

corners and clung to the fractured stones, alive with a cold, hungry expectation. The air was damp enough to taste—iron and brine, with an undercurrent of rotting seaweed. I followed the thin beam of Kas's flashlight, each step down the collapsed nave disturbing a miniature landslide of gravel and sodden leaf litter.

Our breaths sounded too loud, ghosting through the air in small clouds. Pippy pressed herself into the side of my neck, her nails digging in for purchase. Batty clung to the collar of Kas's shirt, wings hunched tight, every so often letting out a high, almost inaudible whine.

We advanced deeper, the distant crash of surf outside echoing through the ribcage of the stonework. Each archway we passed was more ragged than the last, as if something had gnawed at the building from within. The altar sat at the far end, a moss-eaten monolith half buried under the rubble of the collapsed ceiling and the encroaching earth.

Kas paused, scanning the space with a predator's patience. "You feel that?"

"Like someone's watching," I whispered. "Or like the walls themselves are listening."

He nodded, jaw tightening. He pressed the flashlight into my hand and crouched to examine the muddy flagstones, fingertips brushing aside a carpet of mold and dead lichen. "If Calrix hid the amulet here, it'll be warded up to hell and back."

The spell in the air was nothing I've ever felt before. This was old magic—ugly, predatory, desperate. I edged toward the altar, watching Kas's back as he swept the area, his magic already out in silent, invisible waves.

Pippy's small nose twitched at the air, and she uttered a warning squeak. I patted her gently, even as my hands trembled. The closer we got, the more the sense of pressure built. The altar looked like a single, upthrust knuckle, black basalt streaked with white fossil scars and a thick coat of emerald moss. Rainwater pooled in the sunken cup of its top surface.

"Here." Kas pointed to a seam at the base where the stone didn't quite meet the floor. "There's a cavity."

He planted his feet, braced his hands on the altar, and heaved. The stone refused to budge, but he growled, eyes flickering with the faintest glint of psychokinetic power. The altar shuddered, then slid an inch, revealing a hollow beneath just wide enough to reach in.

Kas knelt and fished in his pack, extracting a thin-bladed knife and a bandanna. "Just in case," he said, nodding at my outstretched hands. "If it's booby-trapped, it'll want blood or a life force draw. Or both."

I huffed a bitter laugh. "That's supposed to reassure me?"

He only grinned, sharp and humorless, as I knelt beside him. My pulse thudded. I wiped my palms against my jeans, then wormed my left arm into the narrow opening, cold mud oozing up to my wrist. *Ew.*

It took three blind passes before my fingertips brushed something cold and hard. I fumbled, heart hammering, then curled my fingers around the object and yanked it free. Mud and water sluiced over my knuckles as I pulled out a fist-sized stone amulet, faceted like a massive gemstone and wreathed in a tangle of corroded silver wire.

Kas exhaled hard. "That's it."

The amulet was impossibly cold, sucking the warmth from my palm. I turned it over, heart skipping as I recognized the two-family crest—Ingram's moonflower twined with the Ward's broken spear, pressed into the face of the gem. The twin sigil glimmered with a faint, iridescent sheen even in the darkness.

A tremor ran through the ruins, the sound more

felt than heard. I jerked my head up. The surf outside had grown louder, the rhythm of the sea overlay with a deeper, more urgent pulse.

"Mercy," Kas said, voice sharp with warning.

Just as the words left his mouth, the air exploded into motion. Water jetted from cracks in the flagstones, geysers of salt and sand that hammered the altar and the floor around us. My whole body seized as the first wave slammed into my side, hurling me across the nave. My shoulder cracked hard against a fallen pillar, pain lighting up my vision in white spikes.

I tasted blood, warm and coppery, at the back of my throat. The amulet was still in my grip, its chill numbing out the burn where salt water had eaten through my sleeve and onto my forearm. The skin there sizzled with chemical cold, red and blistering, as if I'd poured acid over it.

Kas's psychokinesis surged—his arms lifted in a crossed block, a bubble of pressure bending the water away from his body. He lunged for me, boots slipping on the film of seawater already pooling on the floor.

The next blast of water caught us both, and this time there was no grace in Kas's shield. We tumbled together into a heap, both scrambling for purchase as the amulet screeched in my hand. My vision tunneled, the world reduced to wet, stinging pain and the relentless howl of the wind.

The psychic echo was a knife blade against my mind. It sliced through the chaos, a voice so warped and static-laced that for a split second I thought I'd gone deaf. "*You cannot unbind what I have cursed,*" it whispered, not in my ear but in the hollow behind my eyes.

I clawed for Kas's arm and found it, dug my nails in, and tried to keep my head above the torrent. "She's here," I croaked. "She's in my head—she's everywhere."

Kas rolled, using his whole body to cover mine. "Focus, Mercy. Channel it. You're stronger than her."

Another jet of water crashed down, flattening us against the jagged stones. My teeth rattled. The amulet writhed in my hand, its power hungry, ugly. I remembered Nina's words: *don't merge your magic with another's until you find the catalyst.* I didn't care. Kas was the only thing keeping me from slipping under.

I reached for the core of my power, the elemental well at my center. My vision flickered, silver streaks crawling into the blue of my eyes. I summoned air in the room, condensing into a razor-thin layer between us and the deadly pressure of the water.

Kas seized on my intent, his own magic twining with mine. The floor beneath us buckled, stone slabs shoving up to create a momentary shelter. We huddled there, our bodies pressed together, as the water raged around us, sluicing away the silt and grit in massive, tearing sheets.

The amulet screamed again. My skin felt like it was peeling away, the saltwater eating down to nerve and bone. I bit my tongue to keep from blacking out.

The psychic voice punched through my mind again. This time, it was edged with triumph. "*You will break. Your line will end with you.*"

Kas leaned in, his forehead resting against mine. His breath was hot and desperate. "Don't let go," he said, more animal than man. "You're not alone. I've got you."

I clamped down on the amulet, my entire focus pouring into that tiny hellish stone. I called on every bit of will I had left, forced the air to slice apart the next wave before it could drown us. Kas's shield flexed, took the brunt, and the stones above groaned, threatening to collapse.

"We need to get out," I gasped. "Now."

Kas nodded, lips drawn tight. He shifted, rolling

us both to our knees, and planted his feet. His left arm went around my waist, the other held out to push the water aside. We half-ran, half-crawled through the wreckage, the amulet's weight dragging at my injured arm.

Pippy clung to my hair, yowling. Batty swooped overhead, dodging jets of water as he scouted our path. The exit arch loomed ahead, warped and distorted through the haze of seawater and pain.

We barreled through, the last blast of salt spray catching us at the threshold and hurling us out onto the rocky ground beyond. I landed hard, scraping my palms open on the wet shale. The cool night air hit my lungs like a punch, but I was alive, and the amulet was still gripped in my fist.

The ruins behind us shuddered, then settled, the magic inside spent for now. Kas pulled me to my feet, steadied me when I wobbled.

"Are you—?" He broke off, seeing the state of my arm. "Shit. Mercy, you're bleeding."

I looked down, surprised to see the raw, puffy red of the burn, streaked with dirt and blood. The pain was almost an afterthought now, eclipsed by the awful, sucking exhaustion that came with using too much magic at once.

"It's fine," I lied. "We got what we came for."

He eyed me, unconvinced, but didn't argue. Instead, he helped me to the SUV, removing his shirt and pressing it to my arm as he dug through the glove box for a first aid kit. I let him fuss, let him clean and bind the wound, even as every nerve ending screamed with the sting of saline and adrenaline crash.

When we were both reasonably patched, he started the engine and peeled away from the ruins, the dark pressing in at the windows again. I cradled the amulet in my lap, the cool of the stone soaking through the denim and into my bones. It hummed, not with life but with a residual, malevolent energy.

Kas drove one-handed, the other resting on my knee, thumb stroking a lazy, reassuring circle even as the tension in his shoulders betrayed his worry.

Neither of us spoke until we were halfway home. I stared at the amulet, watching the way its facets caught the dashboard lights. Purple shot through with veins of silver and black.

"She knew we were coming," I said at last, my voice hoarse. "She's not just haunting the ruins. She's in the magic. In me."

Kas's grip on my knee tightened. "That's what we're counting on. Let her think she's won. We have the amulet now. She can't ascend without it, right?"

I shrugged, too tired for hope. "That's what the journals said. But if she gets to me before we can finish the ritual..."

He shook his head. "No. I won't let that happen."

We pulled into the drive and Kas cut the engine and came around to my side, helping me out of the car, one arm always between me and the empty night.

Inside, I sank into the first chair I found, letting my head fall back and my eyes drift shut. The world narrowed to the steady thump of my pulse and the cold weight of the amulet, still humming in my lap like a curse.

Pippy licked at the raw skin of my arm, her tiny tongue surprisingly gentle. I ruffled her ears, managing a ghost of a smile. Batty landed on the back of the chair, crowding in close with a soft, inquisitive chirp.

Kas hovered, pacing the length of the kitchen, his silhouette cut out by the thin moonlight seeping through the windows. "Tomorrow. We finish this."

I nodded, not trusting myself to speak. The aftershocks of the ward's magic still rippled through my body, each one a reminder that Calrix's curse was not some abstract horror but a living threat. A hungry shadow, clawing at the thin barrier that separated me from oblivion.

But I had the amulet. And for the first time since this nightmare began, I felt a thin thread of resolve tangle through the fear.

Let Calrix come. We'll be ready and we won't be alone.

7

The amulet gleamed dully on the coffee table, its surface still beaded with droplets of seawater. I hunched on the couch, gingerly dabbing ointment on the angry red weal seared into my forearm. The skin was hot and tight, pulsing in time with the sick throb behind my temples. All I wanted was to crawl into bed and pull the covers over my head, to block out the horror of the past few hours. But there was work still to be done.

Kas walked back into the room, meeting my gaze instantly. "The wards are up. I've layered every protection I know. It should buy us some time."

"But not enough," I whispered. After what we'd seen, what we'd heard in the ruins of a chapel. Calrix was coming, and no mere ward would keep her at bay for long.

Kas' jaw clenched, a muscle jumping in his cheek. "No," he agreed grimly. "She knows we have the amulet now. She'll come for it, and for you. It's only a matter of time."

I suppressed a shudder, setting aside the ointment with hands that shook only slightly. The pain in my arm flared and ebbed, but I pushed it down, forced myself to focus. "Then we need to be ready. We need a plan."

Kas scrubbed a hand over his face, his shoulders slumping as he finally ceased his restless pacing. With a sigh, he crossed to join me on the couch, the ragged cushions dipping beneath his weight. For a moment, neither of us spoke, both staring at the seemingly innocuous lump of metal winking malevolently in the lamplight.

I couldn't believe something so small could be the lynchpin of centuries of suffering, the vessel for a curse that even now pulsed through my veins like a living thing. I wanted to snatch it up and hurl it into the fireplace, to watch it melt and deform into slag. But I knew it would do no good. The curse was more than mere metal and hinge - it was old magic, a malevolence that had endured for generations, biding its time.

Biting my lip, I reached for Elara's journal where it lay half-buried under a pile of discarded spell scrolls. The leather was buttery-soft beneath my fingertips, warmed by the heat of the lamps. Gingerly, I flipped it open, skimming over the cramped script until I found the page I sought.

"There," I murmured, my nail scoring the rough parchment. "A 'Vessel of Binding.' Elara mentions it here, in her account of Calrix's original blood rite."

Kas leaned over my shoulder, his brow furrowing as he scanned the faded ink. "An alabaster vial," he read slowly, "filled with the sorceress's own tainted blood. Used to seal the curse and bind it to our lines."

I nodded, a strange calm settling over me as the pieces clicked into place. "The same curse she's been siphoning power from all these years, letting it grow fat on our magic and misery." My voice hardly shook at all. "She intends to use it to fuel her own dark ascension."

Understanding flickered like lightning in Kas' eyes, chased by a grim sort of satisfaction. "But she'll need the vial again to complete the ritual," he said, his tone hardening with resolve. "Without it, her plan crumbles."

"Exactly." I closed the journal with a snap, a fierce, reckless hope kindling in my chest. "And I'd bet that vial is squirreled away in the most secure place Calrix could devise."

Kas' lips twitched, a ghost of his old rakish humor surfacing despite the direness of our straits. "The Ward family vault," he supplied, the words rolling off his tongue like a judge's sentence. "My family's dirty little secret."

I managed a thin smile of my own, the first that had touched my lips since the chapel. "Always knew your family was a bunch of magic hoarders," I teased, bumping his knee with my own.

He snorted, a sound somewhere between amusement and exhaustion. But when he looked at me again, his eyes were flinty with something harder than mirth, sharper than simple determination.

"If the vial's there, we'll find it," he promised, his voice ringing with quiet conviction. "We'll yank the teeth from this curse and ram them down Calrix's scheming throat."

I breathed out a shaky laugh, reaching up to cup his stubbled jaw in my palm. "Have I mentioned lately how much I love it when you get all vengeful and bloodthirsty?" I murmured, only half-joking.

Something darker than humor rippled in his

onyx gaze, a heat that had nothing to do with wrath or reckoning. His hand came up to cover my own, long fingers wrapping around my wrist. "Careful, Mercy," he rumbled, his lips barely brushing my own. "Keep saying things like that, and I might drag you off to bed to show you just how...inspired I can get."

For a moment, I was sorely tempted to let him do just that—to lose myself in his touch, his taste, until the horror and hurt of the night dissolved like mist beneath the rising sun. With a regretful sigh, I pulled back, my fingers slipping from his grasp. "Hold that thought," I murmured, my smile tinged with genuine regret. "Right now, we have a heist to plan."

Kas followed my gaze to Elara's journal, still lying open on the table like an unspoken accusation. When he turned back to me, his half-lidded eyes were hard as chips of obsidian, his sensual mouth firming into a bleak slash. "Tomorrow," he said, a vow and a prayer tangled together on his tongue. "We hit the vault tomorrow and pray we're not too late."

I swallowed around the sudden tightness in my throat. Wordlessly, I leaned into him, resting my cheek against the solid thrum of his heartbeat. Tomorrow, we would beard the beast in its lair, and steal back the hope Calrix had tried so hard to quench.

8

The glass windows of Ward Industries building in Moonbeam Cove caught the early sunlight and scattered it in razor-bright shards across the empty lot. We drove into the underground parking garage. The town above had just stirred, but down here the world still felt half-dreamed and raw.

Kas killed the engine and let the silence settle. For a moment, it was just the rhythmic tick of the Range Rover's cooling engine and the wet metallic taste of anticipation in my mouth. Batty unhooked himself from his custom magical seatbelt and swoop to Kas's headrest. Pippy crawled over my seat to sit in my lap, nose already twitching.

"Ready?" I asked, my voice barely above a whisper, though we both knew there was no one here to hear us.

Kas's mouth quirked, but his eyes had already gone narrow and sharp. "We're as ready as we'll ever be."

We took the stairs two at a time, the familiars already scouting ahead. The lobby had the impersonal shine of all corporate spaces, but here the art installations hummed with dormant threat. Canvases smeared with glow-in-the-dark sigils—none of the playful, homespun ones you'd see in a cottage or a shop, but hard-edged geometrics, their lines vibrating faintly with contained energy. Holo-runes rotated in glass cubes on every side table, each one broadcasting the building's security status in a slow, hypnotic pulse.

The building had a stillness that spoke of wealth and magic and a deep, stubborn arrogance. Nobody expects a break-in at seven a.m. on a Saturday. Okay, we weren't breaking since Kas was the co-owner of Ward Industries.

Pippy scurried down the hall, white fur a blur against the charcoal tiles, while Batty flew ahead of her. Together they made a silent recon team, scouting every blind spot and dead zone the human mind could overlook. The familiarity of the pattern soothed something inside me, even as the adrenaline in my blood. This was the part of my life that made the rest of it feel bearable. I'd never let anyone down on a job, and I wasn't about to start now.

At the first junction, we paused. Kas tilted his head, listening to something I couldn't hear. His hand hovered above a discreet palm reader inset into the wall. He hesitated for a moment, then pressed his hand to it. The door clicked open, then he stepped back for me to enter.

The corridor dead-ended at a slatted steel door. Kas stepped up and opened the door to a maintenance closet lined with racks of rune-etched circuit boards and backup batteries. The air tasted like cold ozone and static, and the only light came from the razor-thin LEDs inside the server cabinets.

Pippy was already nosing at a mesh bin beneath the central rack, tail in the air. I joined her, squinting to see what had caught her attention. There, half-buried under a coil of fiber-optic cable, was a folded slip of vellum so thin it nearly vanished into the shadows.

I palmed the note and opened it. The writing was the same looping script I'd seen in Elara's journals and, more recently, in the margin notes of every cursed artifact we'd tracked.

I squinted, lips moving as I read aloud: "Vial moved to vault B–3. Beware the ink's echo."

Kas, crouched beside me, exhaled slow and hard. "She knows we're coming."

"She's taunting us," I agreed, passing him the note.

His eyes scanned the message and narrowed. "Vault B–3's under two more layers of magical defense. There's a back route through the research floor, but it's littered with sensors—and Calrix has definitely left us a welcoming party."

He didn't sound scared, exactly, but the adrenaline in his voice mirrored my own. He looked at me, and for a second, the whole world shrank to just us and the task at hand.

I tucked the note into my pocket and brushed a hand over Pippy's head. "Let's not keep her waiting."

The corridor outside Vault B–3 felt like the throat of a gun, long and polished and cold. The walls here shimmered with overlapping wards. At the far end stood the vault door.

A faint humming vibrated the air, high and thin and just shy of painful. Kas set his palm against the sigil and closed his eyes. The air around him distorted, a pressure wave that rippled down the hall and rattled the glass in every office for thirty feet. For a second, the bands of copper and obsidian lit up like a slow-motion lightning storm—then Kas spoke the old Ward family word for "Yield," a sound that left my ears ringing, and the runes guttered out.

The first thing I noticed when we entered the vault was the smell. Old iron, ozone, and the sharp, stomach-turning tang of spilled ink. The second thing was the absolute chaos. Shredded parchment littered the concrete. Whole handfuls of blood sigil vials had been swept off the shelves and trampled underfoot. The glass had shattered into knife-edged shards, each glinting with a wet, black-red residue that clung to the edges like congealed wine.

I stepped carefully over the debris and stooped to pick up a sliver of runic-etched crystal. The fragment felt warm in my hand, vibrating faintly with the pulse of a living thing. I turned it over and stared: the mark carved into the curve was unmistakable, a stylized spiral entwined with a serpent's tail.

"This is Calrix's sigil." I turned it to show Kas.

Kas frowned. "She took her own blood vials. Left the rest as a warning."

"Or a challenge," I muttered. The warning in the note—beware the ink's echo—suddenly made more sense. I edged around the perimeter of the room, checking the shelves for anything that might have been overlooked, but every single vial with a Calrix crest had been removed with surgical precision. The rest—hundreds of them—were smashed, the contents pooling and drying in sticky, dark puddles.

"Inventory's up here," Kas said, moving to the digital display embedded in the wall. He thumbed it on, and a readout scrolled through the vault's contents, line by line. "Half the stock is gone. She was quick."

I held up the crystal shard to the light. The runes flickered, catching the dull white LED in a way that revealed a deeper, subtler message—one layer beneath the main sigil, the words "mountain root" etched in nearly invisible micro-script.

"She's moved her lair," I told Kas, not bothering to keep the despair out of my voice. "All the Calrix vials are gone. She's not hiding them—she's taking them somewhere else, probably to finish the binding."

Kas's jaw clenched, a flash of fury tightening every muscle in his face. "Then we cut her off before she gets there."

I stared at the wreckage, the broken glass and drying blood, and felt a slow, implacable anger building in my chest. Calrix wanted to play cat and mouse, but she'd underestimated just how desperate we were. If she needed a confrontation, I'd give her one.

I conjured a map of Moonbeam Cove and the surrounding towns. Then I placed the crystal shard with Calrix's sigil. Losing my eyes, I spoke the words for a location spell. Instantly, a spot on the map, high in the mountains, lit up.

I meet Kas's gaze and he nodded, his hand finding mine with bruising urgency. "Let's finish this."

9

The sun slashed through the windshield in blinding, golden bars, ricocheting off the Range Rover's hood as we barreled up the old logging road. My heartbeat trailed the rhythm of the tires crunching over gravel and pinecones.

I thumbed at the runic shard in my lap, the one we'd snatched from the wreckage of the vault. My intuition told me we might need it.

The final Kas stopped and killed the engine, and for a second the silence pressed in—thicker than the dense trees surrounding the area. I counted four distinct bird calls and the distant drone of a river.

We climbed out. My boots hit the mud with a wet squelch, and the cold, wet air slapped me awake.

I took a deep breath and let the wildness of the place wash over me.

Pippy took the lead as usual, darting up the embankment. Kas followed, and I trailed, running my hands along the peeling bark of the trees, trying to feel for any hidden wards or traps. The terrain got rougher, studded with boulders slicked with emerald moss. The world here was so alive it practically vibrated—each leaf and root thrumming with an energy.

We rounded a thicket of mountain laurel to an opening in the rock face. Water trickled down from somewhere above, splitting into a half dozen miniature.

Pippy hesitated at the threshold. I knelt beside her, brushing a hand down her back. "You sure you want to go in?"

She gave me a sidelong glare that translated to "*are you stupid? Of course I do*", then disappeared into the darkness. Kas went next, ducking his head and sliding sideways through the slot. Batty hovered at the opening, wings trembling, before shooting in after him.

After a brief hesitation, I went in. For a moment, I was blind. I could feel the space opening up around me, a vault of pure night, until Kas's voice drifted back from up ahead.

"Mercy. Over here."

I followed his voice, letting my hand trail along the damp wall. The air was shockingly cold, but dry. Kas waited in a shallow alcove, flashlight in hand. The faint light painted everything in shades of bruise and frost. Batty hung from a stalactite above, and Pippy sniffed circles at the edge of the glow, making a low, throaty noise that was almost a growl.

I scanned the space, searching for anything out of place. The floor was packed mud, but in the center, someone had swept it clean. In a perfect spiral, runes arced out from a central point, drawn in what looked disturbingly like dried blood. The marks were newer than the rest, their edges sharp and clean, as if someone had carved them with a surgeon's hand.

He didn't answer. He just reached for my hand and placed it, palm down, at the edge of the spiral. "Feel that?"

I closed my eyes and reached out with my magic. At first, there was nothing—then a slow, mounting pressure, like someone kneeling on my chest. It pulsed in time with my heartbeat, growing tighter, then looser, then tight again. Underneath it all was a whisper, threading through the air like spider silk.

*You're not alone. You're not alone. You're not alone.*_

I yanked my hand back and scrubbed it against my jeans. "That's the same frequency as the curse. The exact same." I felt it every time my magic flared uncontrollably.

Kas's expression went blank for a second, then he nodded. "Then she's here. Or she was, very recently."

Batty's voice slashed through the quiet, panicked. "Incoming."

We both tensed. Pippy darted for the shadows, stood on her hind legs, and flattened herself against the wall.

Footsteps echoed from the blackness of the tunnel ahead. A silhouette resolved in the lantern's glow—tall, hooded, the hem of her cloak dark as void. Her hands were empty, but her presence filled the entire cave, sucking the warmth from the air. Her voice was static and velvet. "You've brought the amulet. Good." She smiled, though her face was mostly hidden. "I was afraid you'd make me chase you all over this miserable island."

Kas stepped forward, blocking her line to me.

"You're not finishing your ritual, Calrix. Not here, not anywhere."

She didn't flinch. "You don't even know what I'm *trying* to finish, Kasper Ward. You never have. You're so busy playing protector, you've never stopped to ask why your family is worth protecting."

I wanted to tell her to go jump off a cliff, but the words jammed up in my throat. Instead, I gripped the amulet until the metal bit into my hand and forced my voice steady.

"Give up, Calrix. Or we'll—"

She raised one hand, and the runes on the floor surged to life. Crimson light flooded the corridor, illuminating the walls with dancing, unnatural shadows. The sound that came next was a scream, but it didn't come from anyone's mouth. It vibrated in my teeth, in the roots of my hair, in the deepest, oldest parts of my soul.

Kas's knees buckled. He caught himself with one hand, eyes squeezed shut.

Pippy shrieked. The sound was small, but it sliced through the noise like a blade. She darted into the circle, skittering around Calrix's legs, and snapped her jaws on something at the center of the floor.

A vial, stoppered with a small cork and black wax.

Calrix's eyes went wide. For the first time, I saw her flinch. "No!" she hissed, and lunged for Pippy.

I didn't think. I hurled the amulet at her, pouring every scrap of magic I had into the throw. The air rippled—time seemed to stall out, every second stretching into a long, thin thread.

The amulet hit the edge of the circle and detonated with a sound like thunder underwater. The runes on the floor guttered out, and for one glorious instant, the cave went silent. Pippy rolled out of the way, the vial clutched in her tiny mouth, heading out of the cave. Batty streaked down from the ceiling and raked Calrix across the face with a wingtip. She staggered, blood blooming on her cheek, and the hood fell back.

Her face was beautiful, and impossibly old. Her eyes burned with silver fire, but the rest of her features were sculpted from tragedy—high cheekbones, a mouth made for smiling but set in a line of permanent disappointment.

She wiped the blood away with the back of her hand, then laughed. "You're clever, Mercy. But you're not nearly as clever as you think."

She vanished. Just blinked out of existence,

leaving only a swirl of shadow and the dying echo of her laughter.

For a long moment, no one moved.

Pippy staggered back into the cave, dropping the vial at my feet. It rolled to a stop, gleaming darkly in the lantern light.

Kas pushed himself upright, face slick with sweat. "Are you okay?"

I didn't trust myself to speak. I just nodded, then knelt to pick up the vial. It was cold, colder than the cave, colder than anything I'd ever touched. My fingers numbed instantly, but I forced them to close around it, refusing to let go.

"We have to get this back home and break the curse."

Kas nodded, his face grim. He scooped up Pippy and tucked her into the crook of his arm, then reached for my free hand.

I tucked the vial deep into my jacket pocket and leaned into Kas as we made our way out of the cave and to the Range Rover.

We'd made it out alive.

For now.

10

Sunrises in Moonbeam Cove were always magical. Today, I drew on that magic and symbol of a new beginning. The grass was dewy and sharp with the mineral bite of overnight rain. I stood in the kitchen with my hands wrapped around a chipped mug of coffee, looking out over the yard and the ocean beyond it, and tried to imagine how it would feel when the curse finally let go. Would I notice it, like a fever breaking, or would it just fade into the background noise of ordinary pain and joy?

Kas had set up the folding chairs in a wide semicircle, facing the battered old picnic table we'd commandeered as an altar. Someone—Evie, probably—had draped the table in a length of blue velvet that glittered like the inside of a geode. Even through the window I could see the shimmer of it, a promise of ceremony and order. The rest of the ritual tools sat stacked and ready: candles, bowls of salt, a bundle of white sage from Row's garden, and Carlix's vial of blood.

Kas moved through the yard with the restless grace of a caged cat, checking the perimeter, testing the circle's edge with small bursts of psychokinetic force. Each time he tested the ward with his magic, the air around it shimmered, then snapped back into focus. He'd spent half the night laying the protections, and I could feel the drain in his movements—the way his shoulders hunched, the impatience that bled into every gesture.

Pippy and Batty were already in their element. Pippy had claimed a spot at the table's edge, where she was systematically investigating each of the ritual ingredients, sniffing and batting at anything that glittered or rattled. Batty hung upside-down from the eaves, his gaze trained on the unfolding activity below, wings curled up tight like a shroud.

I finished my coffee and rinsed out my cup. As soon as I stepped out the back door, Row pulled into the yard and parked. She was barefoot and radiant, her platinum hair braided into a crown around her head. She carried a basket of something

—muffins, I realized as she set it on the table and shot me a look that dared me to object. "Fortification," she said. "If we're doing this at sunrise, I demand carbs."

Evie and Dani showed up together, Evie in a sundress that looked amazing on her, Dani in her usual jeans and a blazer that looked like it cost more than my car. Andrea trailed after, her composure as chill and precise as ever, but with a warmth in her eyes that made her look almost human. My parents arrived last.

Nina tuned in via scrying orb, a clear quartz spear the size of a softball, on the picnic table, her face distorted in its depths like a goldfish in a bowl. "You look like hell, darling."

"Thanks, Nina," I replied. "You're a vision yourself."

She cackled, then immediately coughed. "Let's get this over with before my connection drops. The old gods are especially cranky today."

We started the ritual with the grounding chant, all of us standing in a loose circle, hands joined. Row led, her voice clear and sure: "Blood and bond, now be free, By earth and air, by storm and sea."

There was a pause, the kind that stretched and threatened to break. Then Nina's voice sounded through the orb: "Focus on the harm you undo, Mercy, and let your elemental core ring true."

I took a breath, let it expand in my lungs until it pressed against the walls of my chest, and then stepped forward to kneel at the makeshift altar. The grass was wet and cold, and the scent of sage mingled with the ozone left over from Kas's wards. I traced a water-and-air rune in the salt and let my magic bleed out through the tips.

The effect was immediate. A silver mist coiled up from my hands, twining around the driftwood centerpiece. Kas stood behind me, his hands planted on the altar's edge, projecting a pulse of psychokinetic ripples that caught and shaped the mist. Our magics tangled, not in conflict but in a kind of desperate, mutual hunger. I could feel it—the way our energies spun together.

Row's voice was steady behind me. "Hold fast, Mercy. It's working."

But the air had vibrated, a faint, discordant hum that made my molars ache. The mist thickened, swirling faster, shot through with streaks of midnight blue and ugly, bilious green. I recognized the signature instantly—Calrix, pushing back, trying to wrest control.

Then the wind picked up. The salt runes at the

edge of the circle shuddered, and I heard Evie's voice, high and panicked: "She's breaking through!"

Kas grunted, pouring more power into the barrier. "She's not getting in. Not this time."

But Calrix's voice punched through the static, her tone rich with contempt: "Pathetic. You unbind nothing but your own fears." The words warped the air, twisted it into shapes that hurt to look at.

Andrea and Mom moved as one, reinforcing the circle with a counter-chant, their voices blending in a low, resonant hum. I felt the circle firm up, the grass standing rigid, the air growing thick and viscous.

Nina's image in the orb flickered, then sharpened, her eyes wide and wild. "Now, Mercy! Focus on the break—on the curse's root, not the wound it left."

I dug deep, pushing past the pain in my arm, the exhaustion in my bones. I thought of every ancestor who'd suffered under this curse, every day I'd lived with its threat looming over me. I thought of the way it had tried to hollow me out, make me into a vessel for someone else's rage and ambition.

"Go to hell, Calrix."

As I thrust everything I had into the root of the curse inside me, the mist convulsed, splintered, and reformed. The lattice of wind and water cinched tight, squeezing the fragments until they glowed.

But the backlash was brutal. My vision swam, my body jerked backward as if yanked by a hook in my spine. Kas caught me, his arms anchoring me against the next wave of force. For a second, everything went silent except for the frantic hammer of my own pulse.

Then the familiars acted.

Pippy launched herself off the table, streaking toward the edge of the circle. Batty followed, flitting overhead in tight, erratic loops. I caught a flash of movement—a glint of something metallic in the hedge—and realized, too late, that Calrix had agents even here, even now.

Pippy pounced, teeth bared. There was a shriek, the sound of flesh and fabric tearing, and then she rolled away with a small, rune-etched stone in her jaws. Batty swooped down and snatched it up, beating his wings furiously as he darted back to the altar.

Row snatched the stone out of the air, her eyes alight with fierce pride. "Acolyte's ward key," she breathed. "She's using proxies to try to splinter the circle."

Dani and Evie doubled down on their warding,

hands clasped and knuckles white. I felt the ground tremble, the ancient power of the Ward family roots rising to mesh with the Ingram legacy. Together, they hammered the interference flat, pinning it beneath a blanket of raw earth energy. The mist surged once more, almost desperately, then shivered and dissipated.

Row stepped forward, into the center of the circle. She looked at me, then at the rest of my family, and squared her shoulders. "By my heart's true will," she said, "I stand between curse and cure. Set all bloodlines clean."

Her words burned. I could feel the life force she offered, a bright beacon in the swirling dark. The lattice of wind and water flared, then funneled into the bowl on the table. The water glowed, turned to sand, then dissolved.

For a heartbeat, all was still.

Then Calrix's laughter echoed one last time, distorting into a scream of static. A swirl of shadow twisted in the patio's corner, then unraveled, thinning into nothingness. The circle fell silent, the only sound the slow exhale of breath from every person present.

The sky brightened, gold and pink and utterly without malice. I sagged into Kas's arms, the weight of years and curses falling away like a wet coat.

Even the familiars seemed to relax. Pippy curled up on my lap, her sides heaving with the effort of her charge. Batty found a perch on Kas's shoulder, his tiny body vibrating with satisfaction. Both our familiars will sleep the rest of the day and through the night to recharge. They deserved it.

We had done it. The curse was broken.

I didn't cry, not right away. But when Row hugged me, hard and breathless, I felt the tears slip down my cheeks, silent and clean as rain.

Kas wrapped me up in his arms. He didn't say anything—he didn't have to. I felt the tremor in his muscles, the wild rush of relief and disbelief that flooded through him as the reality of what we'd done set in. I leaned into the warmth, the solidity, the fact that after everything, we were both still here.

Andrea and Mom reached us at the same time. Mom enveloped me in a hug that threatened to break my ribs, her cheek pressed wet and hot against mine. Andrea grabbed Kas in a bone-crushing embrace, then pulled me in as well, her usual composure washed out by the rawness of the moment.

"Proud of you," she whispered, her voice so soft I almost missed it.

Nina's scrying orb glowed on the table, the image inside flickering but steady. "It's done," she said. "The curse is gone." Then her eyes narrowed, and her voice dropped a half-octave. "But you've awakened something new. There's always a cost, Mercy. Be wary of what comes next."

I nodded, not trusting myself to speak. The backyard looked transformed. The grass glistened in the morning light, every blade standing tall and electric. Even the battered picnic table seemed to glow, as if the ritual had bled the stains and scars out of the wood and replaced them with something cleaner, truer.

Evie and Dani took a seat on the steps, their shoulders pressed together, laughing in the soft, wild way you do when you've just survived the impossible. Row and I caught each other's gaze, and for a second the world seemed to shrink to just us. She smiled, tired but luminous, and mouthed, "You did it."

I shook my head, grinning. "We did."

Pippy and Batty basked in the glow of a post-battle victory. Pippy dozed in a patch of sun, her fur already fluffed and dry, while Batty performed lazy, triumphant loops around the edge of the yard. Obviously not ready to crash yet. Now and then, he let out a joyful shriek, a sound so pure I couldn't help but laugh.

Row was the first to break the spell. "If anyone needs me, I'll be in the kitchen hoarding muffins before Kas's bottomless pit gets them all." She winked at Kas, who rolled his eyes but didn't deny the accusation.

Mom drifted over and wrapped Row in a hug, whispering something in her ear that made Row snort and nod. Andrea followed. They moved toward the house, their voices fading into the hush of the morning as they went. Nina's orb dimmed and blinked out, leaving only a faint shimmer in the air.

Kas and I lingered in the yard. The silence felt different now, expectant rather than oppressive. I watched him run a hand through his hair, felt the way his fingers trembled with spent adrenaline. He caught me looking and shrugged. A half-apology, half-celebration.

"You know what the best part is?" he said.

I shook my head, smiling. "Enlighten me."

"No one's trying to kill us. Not right now, anyway." He grinned, and for the first time in weeks, it didn't look forced.

I laughed, the sound low and giddy. "Give it a minute."

He pulled me in for another hug, softer this time, his chin tucked over my shoulder. "We made it, Mercy," he murmured. "Whatever comes next, we made it."

I closed my eyes and let the words settle, let myself believe them.

Inside, the familiars had taken over the kitchen. Pippy hopped from counter to counter, systematically exploring every mug and bowl within reach. She fished a sugar cube out of a chipped teacup and scurried away with it, tail whipping behind her like a streamer. Batty hung upside-down from the pot rack, batting at a dangling sachet of chamomile with delicate, surgical precision.

Row had made good on her threat; half the muffin basket was gone, the other half in mortal peril. She lounged at the table, feet propped on the next chair, a mug of coffee balanced in the crook of her elbow. Evie and Dani had claimed the window seat, their heads bent together over a phone, giggling as they scrolled through whatever they were looking at.

Andrea and Mom hovered near the stove, their voices low but happy. Andrea poured herself a cup of tea and shot me a glance, the barest hint of a smile on her lips. "I'll admit it," she said. "I had my doubts. But you pulled it off."

Mom squeezed my hand. "Your grandmother would have been so proud."

I ducked my head, cheeks burning. "Thanks. I just... I didn't want anyone else to get hurt."

Dani raised her mug in salute. "To no more casualties."

"Or drama," Evie added, then immediately snorted. "Okay, maybe just less drama."

The doorbell rang, three sharp chimes that cut through the noise. I set my mug down and wiped my hands on my jeans, already bracing for whatever weirdness Moonbeam Cove wanted to throw at us next.

Row trailed after me to the front door, curiosity shining in her eyes. "If it's a cult recruiter, I'm answering."

I shushed her and cracked the door. On the stoop sat a plain brown package, no return address, just my name. The handwriting made my skin crawl; I knew it, but couldn't place it.

I bent down and picked up the box. It was lighter than it looked, rattling faintly when I shook it. No ticking, no obvious curses, but the hairs on my arms stood straight up.

Row whistled, low and impressed. "Somebody's got your number."

I carried it inside, set it on the kitchen table, and eyed it like it might explode. Kas joined us, his brow furrowed. "You expecting a delivery?"

"Nope," I said, popping the tape with a knife. The box opened with a sigh, and inside was a single sheet of thick, gray paper, folded in half.

I pulled it out. The paper was heavy, almost fabric, and covered in a sharp, angular rune drawn in violet ink. The rune glowed faintly, pulsing in time with my heartbeat.

Row leaned in. "That's not in Elara's journal."

Kas took the page, squinting at the symbol. He pulled out his phone and opened an app, switching to night vision. The rune flared, casting a web of secondary lines across the kitchen table.

"Blood sigil magic," he said. "But not Calrix's. Someone else is borrowing her style."

Batty landed on the back of Kas's chair, eyes narrowed. "That's a warning," he said, voice pitched low. "Or a promise."

Pippy slunk out from under the table and perched on my foot, nose twitching furiously. She didn't seem afraid—more like she was waiting, poised to spring at whatever came next.

I unfolded the paper. Scrawled across the center, in the same jagged script, were the words: "Congratulations on breaking the bond curse. Now prepare for your next battle."

My stomach lurched. The phrase felt wrong, oily and cold. But beneath the dread, something else—curiosity, the faintest shimmer of hope.

Kas wrapped an arm around my shoulders. "Whatever it is, we'll handle it."

Row grinned, baring her teeth. "Hell yeah, we will."

I laughed, a small, unsteady sound. "I guess it's true what they say. No rest for the wicked."

* * *

I hope you enjoyed book two of Mercy and Kas's story. Find out what happens next in book 3, A Bitter Brew of Magic

Don't forget to leave a review!

ABOUT LIA DAVIS

USA Today bestselling author Lia Davis spends most of her time writing witty paranormal women's fiction and urban fantasy, the majority of which takes place in fantasy worlds full of magic and mayhem. She prides herself on her ability to craft strong and sassy heroines, emotionally intelligent alpha heroes, and rich, expansive universes that readers want to visit again and again.

She is the mastermind behind the bestselling Ashwood Falls Series and the co-author of the beloved Witching After Forty Series.

She currently resides in Florida where she's working on her very own happily-ever-after with her supportive husband and spends her free time doting on a pack of feisty felines and her loving family.

Lia is represented by Amanda Wooden at SBR Media Literary Agency

Linktree: https://linktr.ee/authorliadavis

ALSO BY LIA DAVIS

Paranormal Women's Fiction /Para-Cozy Mysteries

Witching After Forty (Co-written with L.A. Boruff)

Fanged After Forty (Co-written with L.A. Boruff)

Hunting After Forty (Co-written with L.A. Boruff)

Shifting Through Midlife (Co-written with L.A. Boruff and Lacey Carter)

Mercy Ingram Mysteris

Paranormal Romance Series

Shifters of Ashwood Falls

Bears of Blackrock

Dark Scales Division (Co-written with Kerry Adrienne)

Shifting Magick Trilogy

The Divinities

Coven's End (Co-written with L.A. Boruff)

Academy's Rise (Co-written with L.A. Boruff)

Urban Fantasy Series

Randi Sanderson Series

Made in the USA
Columbia, SC
28 July 2025

60990603R00065